PIPER SKY, "THE COACH'S DAUGHTER" PRESENTS:

PIPER SKY'S PINK POPSICLE SHOES

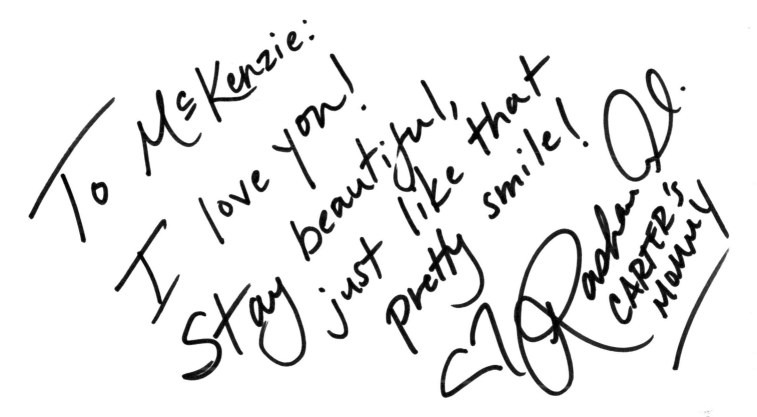

To McKenzie:
I love you!
Stay beautiful,
just like that
pretty smile!
Rashan Ali:
CARTER'S Mommy

WRITTEN BY: RASHAN ALI
ILLUSTRATED BY: AHAD PACE

Piper Sky's Pink Popsicle Shoes
ISBN: 978-0-9831695-8-1
Written by: Rashan Ali
Illustrations by: Ahad Pace
The illustrations were done by Atlanta based artist, Ahad Pace, who is an established
graphic designer and a fine artist as well. Visit him online at ahadpace.com.

A New Day — Publishing

Published by: A New Day Publishing www.anewdaybooks.com

Dedication

Heavenly Father, thank you for your grace.

To my husband Brian, you are my light.
Bailey and Carter you are my reason and motivation.

Mommy, thank you for sculpting the dream.

Daddy, you are the vessel for the gift.

Colin Godfrey: my brother, my friend.

Jen Price, because you've been there.

Special thanks to my circle of Moms: Deanna Godfrey,
Stacy Frazier, Crystal Worthem, Micki Havard, Sheri Riley,
Jessica Pedraza and Tracy Nicole.

Sonia Murray, for making me go deeper.

Dawn Nuriddin, your diligence and insight saved me. I'm forever
grateful.

For little girls who never saw themselves before, this is for you.

"Look how far I can kick that ball! I jump so high, I can even touch that stop sign! I run as fast as a track star!

I'm Piper Sky, The Coach's Daughter and my Pink Popsicle Shoes
make me do some amazing things in this town of Terrantodd!"

Piper Sky loved her Pink Popsicle Shoes so much that she wished she could wear them forever. Those shoes had the shiniest purple, orange and green rhinestones. They even had popsicles stitched on the flap. She absolutely adored them!

All of Piper Sky's friends wanted to wear her spectacular shoes. She wanted to share them, but there was only one way she would give her friends that chance. It was really simple, but only Piper knew the secret.

One day, Piper Sky and her little sister Charly Star were playing in the park. She saw her friend Ella walking toward her carrying two yummy smoothies. Piper Sky loved smoothies!

"Hi Piper! I brought us creamy, strawberry - pineapple smoothies. If I give you one, will you let me wear your pink popsicle shoes?"

Piper calmly answered, "No my friend. I wear these with pride and you know that I won't take any bribes. These shoes have powers I would like to share and those powers are only in this pair."

Ella was very angry and stormed off sipping her tasty smoothie.

Piper Sky waved goodbye and returned to what she enjoyed most, which was having fun with her sister. After playing for a while, she saw Jin from her swim team walking towards them.

"Hello Jin! How are you?" she asked.
"I'm great, but I could be better! I brought your favorite warm, peanut butter cookies and a tall glass of milk. I'll give you my cookies and milk if I can wear your Pink Popsicle Shoes."

Piper Sky smiled and said, "No my friend. I wear these with pride and you know that I won't take any bribes. These shoes have powers I would like to share and those powers are only in this pair."

Jin angrily walked away, eating her warm cookies. She thought Piper Sky was being so mean.

Piper Sky and Charly Star continued to play, but Charly wondered why Piper did not let her friends wear her shoes?

Ella and Jin had offered her a smoothie and her favorite cookies, yet she didn't budge. She knew her sister always loved to share. There must be something really special about those shoes, Charly thought.

After a long day, Piper and Charly headed home. During dinner, their dad (affectionately called Coach) asked about their day. Piper told him about Ella and Jin's gifts. He reminded her, "Always share and never expect anything in return."

"I know Coach, I know."
Piper chuckled.

That night, before they drifted off to sleep, Charly Star asked her sister if she could wear her Pink Popsicle Shoes. Piper Sky answered with a smile, "Sure, little sister. Of course you can!"

Charly Star was surprised. Hadn't Piper refused to let her friends Ella and Jin wear her shoes today? Then Charly smiled. She was sure Piper agreed to let her wear the shoes because they were sisters.

Each year in Terrantodd, there was a huge festival. It was a family fun day with games, races, face-painting, rides and jumpy houses!

Piper Sky and Charly Star were walking toward the colorful jumpy house when they saw Ella and Jin. The girls were surprised to see what Piper's little sister was wearing.

Charly Star was wearing Piper Sky's Pink Popsicle Shoes!

The girls could hardly believe their eyes!!

"Why did you let Charly wear your beautiful pink shoes?" Ella asked. Piper calmly replied, "Because she didn't want anything in return. And most of all, she did not try to bribe me. She just asked politely so I let her wear them."

"That's all she did?! That's the secret!" blurted Jin.
"Yes, the shoes mean a lot to me, but not more than my friends do. The next time you want something from someone, including your friends, just ask!"

The girls hugged and walked over to the jumpy house to play. By the end of the day, Piper Sky gave Ella and Jin a chance to wear her special shoes.

The girls ran faster, kicked harder and jumped higher with Piper Sky's Pink Popsicle Shoes. They were amazed! And the best part was that Piper finally got a chance to share with her friends... all they had to do was ask.

The End!

CPSIA information can be obtained
at www.ICGtesting.com
Printed in the USA
LVIC06n0938210415
435131LV00006B/7